THE GHOST PRISON

THE GHOST PRISON

JOSEPH DELANEY

ILLUSTRATED BY SCOTT M. FISCHER

Cover design by Daniel Pelavin

Published by Sourcebooks Fire, an imprint of Sourcebooks, Inc.
P.O. Box 4410, Naperville, Illinois 60567-4410
(630) 961-3900
Fax: (630) 961-2168
teenfire.sourcebooks.com

Originally published in the United Kingdom by Andersen Press Limited.

Library of Congress Cataloging-in-Publication data is on file with the publisher.

Printed and bound in the United States of America.
MA 10 9 8 7 6 5 4 3 2 1

For Marie

Contents

1

A New Job

"For pity's sake, get up, lad. Do you want to lose the job before you've even started?"

I looked around disoriented, wiping drool from my chin. What time was it? I felt like I'd been in bed no time at all.

"Come on, Billy," Mrs. Hendle said, more kindly this time. "They told you to be there an hour after sunset and it's that time already." She passed me my jacket hanging over the chair and I pulled myself wearily out of bed.

A few of the other lads ran into the room, laughing and jeering, but she soon shooed them away. I could still hear them though, sniggering through the door.

"You gonna be scared up there, Billy?"

"Don't you want to go?"

"Get away with you!" I shouted as I barged through the door, sending them scattering in every direction. Bloomin' brats.

But they were right. I was *bloody* scared. This wasn't the sort of job I'd been hoping for. "Beggars can't be choosers," my old ma used to say, God rest her soul. And she was right. There aren't many jobs that lads from the orphanage can get. I was lucky to have this one. A few more weeks' training and I'd have enough put by to get lodgings elsewhere, move away from this stupid Home for Unfortunate Boys. It would all be worth it in the end.

I jogged down the steps and out into the moonlit streets. As I left the village and ran along the country lanes, I could see the castle up ahead of me and I walked toward it, trying to be brave.

After all, I wasn't going to be imprisoned there. I was just going to work there guarding the prisoners. Those other lads were being silly. Just jealous. It was a job and I was going to do it.

But I knew why they thought I should be scared—why I *was* scared. It was who I'd be guarding that was the problem: murderers, common criminals, and convicted witches. That was my job. Or at least it would be once I'd finished my training.

There was a new moon, slender and horned, soon to be overwhelmed by the dark clouds blustering in from the west. I shivered but not just with cold. I'd heard stories about the castle after dark, about things long dead that walked its damp

corridors. And there wasn't a person alive in the village who hadn't heard the screams coming from there: low, agonizing moaning; wild, hysterical cackles; wretched, mournful sobbing—we'd heard them all.

The building was large and forbidding, set on a high hill about three miles from the nearest town and surrounded by a dense wood of sycamore and ash trees.

It was constructed from dark, dank stone with turrets, battlements, and a foul-smelling moat that was rumored to contain the skeletons of those who had attempted to escape.

I'd never wanted to be on the night shift. But my feelings counted for nothing. Orders were orders, and after just two weeks preliminary training, I'd been told to report one hour after sunset. But being unused to going to bed in the afternoon and finding it hard to nod off in the first place with the other lads around, I'd overslept. I was already more than half an hour late and castle guards were supposed to be punctual.

As I reached the castle and looked up at its menacing walls, there was a clanking, grinding sound and then the portcullis began to rise. They knew I was there. Nobody approached the castle without being noticed.

There were always eyes watching, always people noting your approach.

Behind the portcullis was a huge wooden door studded with iron. It was another five minutes before that opened, and I tried to wait patiently as a light drizzle began to drift into my

Come on, come on, I thought, starting to pace. *I'm late enough already*.

At last, the door started to grind back on its hinges to reveal a burly guard, scratching at the stubbly beard on his face. He scowled at me. "Name?" he demanded.

"Billy Calder," I answered.

He knew my name and I knew his—George Ellerton; he'd been letting me in each day for my training. But he was following the rules. Anyone entering had to identify himself.

"You'll be working under Adam Colne," he said, and my heart sank. I'd heard about Adam Colne during my training. He was a mountain of a man with a reputation for being tough and ruthless. He'd once thrown a trainee guard from the battlements into the moat. The boy had been lucky to survive.

"Mr. Colne's waited over half an hour for you, and he's not best pleased to say the least. I wouldn't like to be in your shoes, boy."

"I'm sorry," I said, "I lost track of time and..."

"Save your excuses for Mr. Colne, lad. Here he comes now." I turned around and saw a huge man, with more hair on his face than his head, marching toward me, a large bunch of keys rattling at his belt.

Colne stared at me hard without blinking, making me feel very nervous. It was the first time we'd met, and I knew I hadn't made a good impression.

"You're late!" he growled. "There are only six guards on the night shift and it's important that we are *all* present. Do you understand me?"

I nodded. My voice had escaped me.

"So it won't happen again, will it, boy?"

This time I shook my head vigorously.

"Those who work for me never make the same mistake twice—not if they want to carry on breathing. You have to know your place in the scheme of things. Do I make myself clear?"

"Yes, sir," I forced myself to answer.

"Good, as long as we've got that straight, I'll forget your lateness and we'll make a fresh start from now. You'll be happy here, boy. We're just like a close-knit family on the night shift."

I didn't know much about families because my parents had died when I was young and I'd spent the last nine years in the orphanage. This was my first job, since I'd turned fifteen and soon I'd be thrown out to make my own way in the world. Yes, I'd been in the village for nine years now, but I still felt like a stranger. I'd never made any friends.

"So first things first," Colne continued. "Do you know why you've been transferred to the night shift?"

"No, sir."

"Someone asked for you. Someone politely requested your presence. Someone we have to keep sweet. 'Let the young Calder boy guard at night,' she begged. Wouldn't you like to know who she is?"

She? I nodded. I hadn't got a clue.

"Then why don't you take a guess?"

Who could it be? There were some female as well as male prisoners in the castle—mostly convicted witches—but certainly no female jailers. The place was run by men. But as far as I was aware, I knew no one imprisoned in this castle—or any castle for that matter.

Then I had a thought. "Is it one of the prisoners, sir? Lizzie Guntripp?"

Lizzie was locked up in the west wing of the castle. She'd been accused of being a witch by her neighbor because all his potatoes got the blight after he ran over her cat with his cart. But I didn't believe she was and neither did half the village. I'd smiled at her during training once and served her a larger portion of gruel. Maybe it was her.

Colne looked at me and laughed. "Lizzie Guntripp? No, we drowned her three days ago. She didn't float, so it seems she was innocent after all—but by the time

we realized, she was dead already. You win some, you lose some." He laughed again coldly.

I looked at my shoes, not wanting to join in with his laughter.

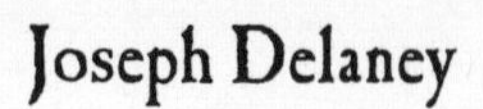

"No, the young lady asking after you is Netty and she *was* one of the prisoners, boy. But she's a prisoner no longer."

That didn't make any sense. If she'd been released, why had she requested my presence on the night shift?

"Where is she now?" I asked.

"Mostly she's to be found in Execution Square. One of her favorite places it is because that's where they hanged her."

My face must have shown my shock. "Netty is a ghost, and we need to keep her sweet or it's bad news for everybody.

"A ghost, sir?" I spluttered. "A ghost and she asked for me?"

He threw back his head and laughed. "Aye, little orphan boy. Seems someone loves you after all."

"Who is she? I mean, who *was* she?" I asked.

"Some call her '*Long-Neck Netty*' on account of how stretched it was by the rope. But don't let her overhear you using that name. She doesn't like it. Even when she's in a good mood, she raps and bangs and wakes up the prisoners. Sometimes she turns the milk sour or gives us nightmares. No, it don't do to cross Netty. So follow me, boy! If it's you she wants on the night shift, it's you she'll get."

And he lifted a lantern and marched off swinging his bunch of keys.

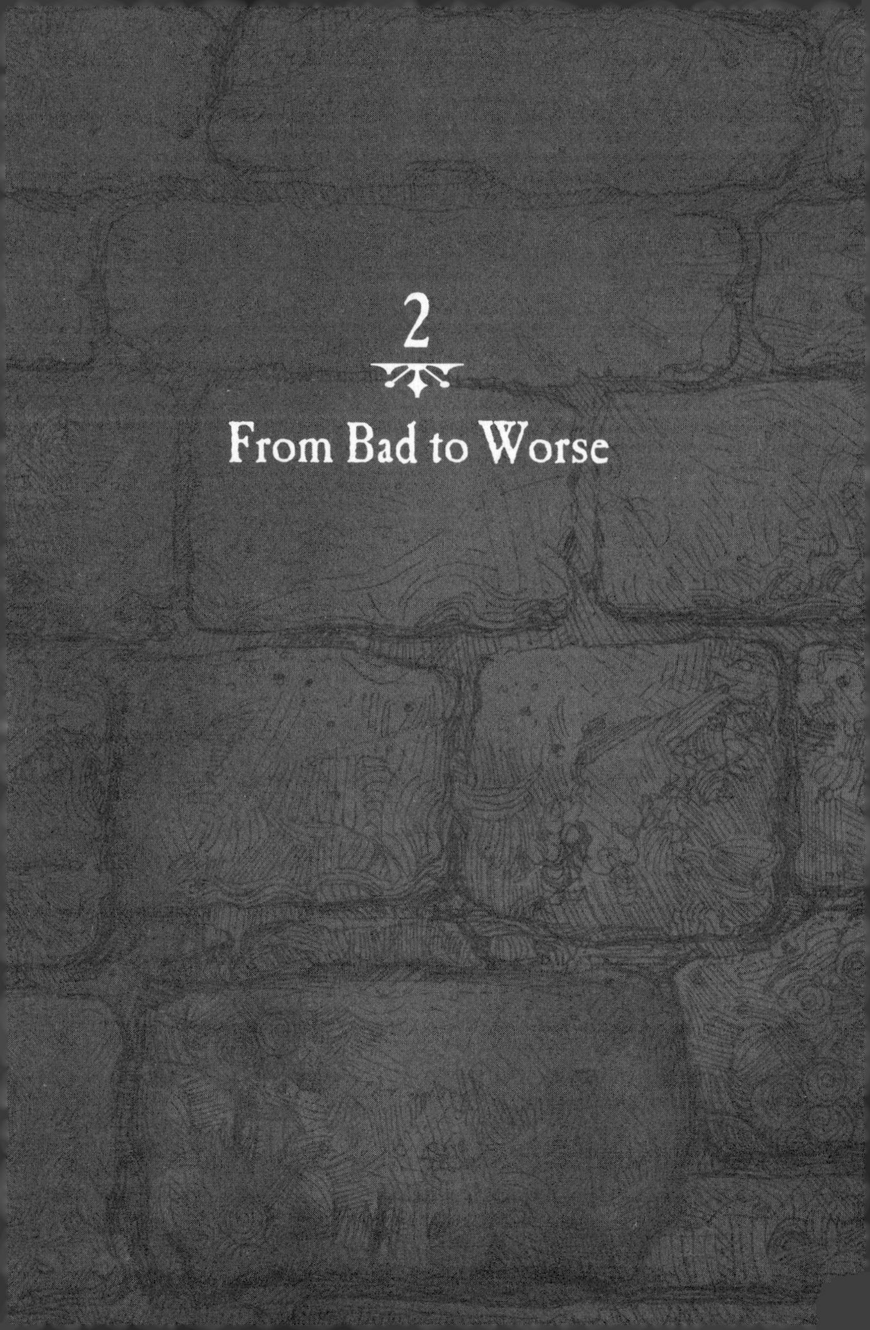

2

From Bad to Worse

I had to jog to keep up with Mr. Colne as I followed him through a tunnel and into the castle yard. A thousand questions were swirling around my head.

"But how does this Netty know who I am, sir?"

"Must have seen you during your training and taken a shine to you."

"Are we going to see her now?" I asked, my knees beginning to tremble. The thought of facing a ghost had suddenly turned me right off

the job. *Why on earth had I applied to be a prison guard in the first place?*

"Nobody goes to see Netty, boy. She comes to see you. No doubt she'll turn up when she's good and ready. Of course, she's not the only ghost who haunts this prison." He pointed up at two cell windows high on the wall. It wasn't time for lights out yet, and they were the only two cells in darkness.

"We never put prisoners in those two cells, boy. Not now anyway. Know why?"

"Are they haunted, sir?"

"They're haunted all right, but by exactly what we're not sure. About ten years ago the castle was filled to bursting with prisoners, so we had to use those two cells. We knew they were supposed to be haunted by something unpleasant, but there were no precise records, so we took a chance and locked two drunken farm hands up for the night. Got into a fight they had and then battered the parish constable who'd tried to separate them.

"The morning after they were trembling like leaves in an autumn storm. And both told the same tale. In the middle of the night, something invisible but very strong had grabbed them by their throats and tried to drag them into the wall. But that weren't all..."

Colne stood there for a while staring into the darkness, shaking his head and muttering to himself as if he were reliving the experience. He seemed to have forgotten all about me.

"What happened?" I pressed him.

"Well, as I said, the castle cells were all occupied, so we had to put them back in the same quarters again the following night. Come dawn we regretted it. In hindsight, we should have sent them off elsewhere to be locked up, but we hadn't the manpower to transport 'em. In the morning one of them was dead. He'd been strangled and there were finger marks embedded in his throat. His eyes were bulging too—it wasn't a pretty sight. But the other had disappeared, or at least most of him had. There was a large pool of blood on the cell floor and in it were his teeth."

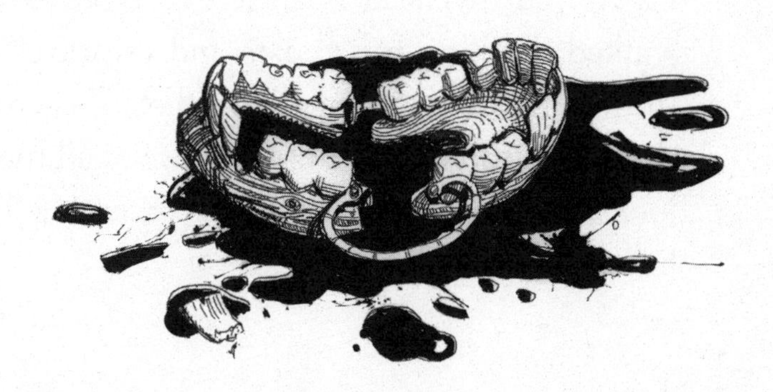

"His teeth? Was that all that was left of him?"

"His dentures, boy, to be precise, which were made out of wood. It seemed that whatever had taken him couldn't get them through the stone wall as well. Flesh and bone, yes, but not Rowan wood. It's a wood that has certain properties. Witches aren't supposed to be able to touch it, and some say it wards off dark apparitions. Anyway, let's get inside, out of this drizzle. I need something to warm my belly."

We passed along two corridors and at the end of each was a sturdy door to be unlocked. I swiveled my head from left to right as we walked, looking for ghosts and creatures of the night. Moving even a short distance across the prison took some time because of all those locks; no wonder each jailer carried a big heavy bunch of keys.

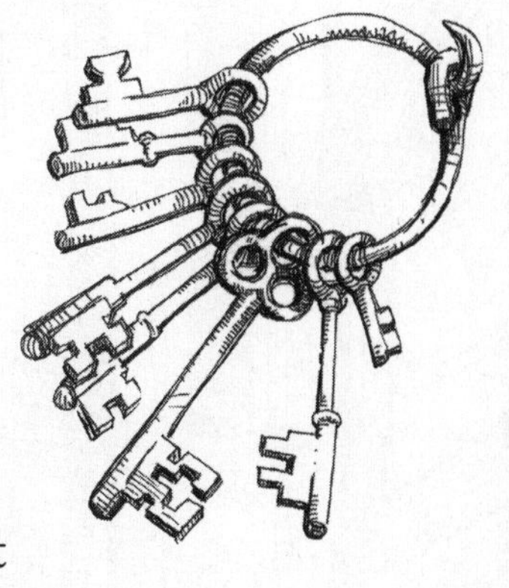

At last we emerged into a large room with a small fire in the grate, three big wooden tables, and lots of chairs.

"This is the quarters for the night shift," Colne said. "Make yourself at home if you want."

I'd never visited the room before because it was always locked during the day. But there was little evidence now to suggest that it was ever occupied. There were no cups, cutlery, or plates on the tabletops. The room was tidy—too tidy. Something about that made me feel rather uneasy. It definitely wasn't somewhere I could feel at home.

"Of course," Colne said, catching the

quizzical look on my face, "we don't use it much. Not a nice room this."

"Is this haunted as well?" I asked. Things seemed to be going from bad to worse. Was nowhere safe in this place?

"By night the whole castle is haunted, boy, but a lot depends on what's doing the haunting. There are some really nasty things that rap and bang in here, so most guards prefer to take their rest in other places."

"Have you heard anything, sir? D'you think it's true?"

He nodded and leaned in closer to me. "About twenty years ago, when I first started on the job, I was braver, much braver, and I sat in here one night eating bread and ham that my wife, Martha, had packed for me. She's dead now, poor soul. It's funny, isn't it? All these castle ghosts but never once did the spirit I most wished to see come back to say farewell." He shook his head sadly and for a moment he didn't seem quite so scary. "Anyway, there I was sitting in that chair over there chewing my food..."

He pointed to a wooden chair nearest the door.

"At last my stomach was full and I started to doze. Then something woke me, lad. A strange noise came from behind me, and I swear to God it raised the hairs on the back of my neck and sent chills running down my spine."

"What was it?" I asked.

"Well, it sounded like something was gnashing its teeth together hard at the same time as growling deep in its throat. But whatever it was, it was small and dark, and it shot past my chair and scuttled across the flags there quicker than I could blink."

I glanced down at the floor expecting to see this evil creature for myself.

"It scared me, boy, I don't mind telling you. I tried to convince myself that it was just a rat, but it had passed straight through a closed door, so I knew that it was something more than that. And there was a smell too—a stench of fire and brimstone. So it was definitely something evil. Something it's better not to think about. Something straight from hell. I rarely eat in here now—at least not when I'm by myself. One funny thing about ghosts is that they're most likely to put in an appearance when you're alone."

He sighed then shook his head. "But there are worse places in this castle and the worst place of all is the one that I have to visit *every* night. And I *have* to visit it alone. It's a place we call *The Witch Well*. There's a prisoner down there that it's best to keep away from. He's tethered to a ring in the dungeon floor by a long chain and sleeps all day, but he is wide-awake after dark. He has to be fed at midnight or things could get really awkward for everybody who works here. Someone has to do that dangerous job and, as the most experienced guard on the night shift, it falls to me. As well as the special prisoner, the well has something else to make it a fearsome place. It's haunted by foul things—the ghosts of those confined there long ago. I only wish I didn't have to go there, but duty is duty."

I couldn't believe what I was hearing. We'd often scared each other in the orphanage with stories of how the castle might be haunted. But it seemed the reality was a good deal worse than our imaginings.

"Cheer up, lad. I'll show you where the well is later—but don't worry, you won't have to go down there. In fact, I'll tell you this now and I don't want you to ever forget it—never go down there if you know what's good for you. I've lost a few good guards down there over the years.

"*Lost* them?"

"Aye," he said, and slapped me on the back. "Lost them." But he didn't seem to want to tell me anymore. "Anyway, I'll make us both a hot drink to ward off the chills of the night. By the looks of it you could do with one."

★

Twenty minutes later, warm milk and honey in our bellies, we set off again and Adam Colne led me through another series of corridors with occupied cells on either side. I found myself running to keep up with his long stride. By now it was after lights out and you could hear the prisoners moaning in their sleep or sometimes crying out as if in the grip of a terrifying nightmare. I'd heard noises similar to this in the orphanage. Nighttime is hard for some of the lads, especially when they first arrive and their mothers still haunt their dreams. But after the awful stories Colne had just been telling me, the moaning of these prisoners chilled me to the bone. How terrible to be trapped here every night—locked in a cell which ghosts were free to enter!

Colne opened then locked each door at the end of the corridors behind us after slamming it with a clang.

"Never leave your keys in the lock, even for a moment, boy," he warned. "Always fasten them back onto your belt. It's the safest way, so nobody else can ever get their hands on them."

At last we ended up in the open again, the drizzle falling straight down onto our heads, the castle walls rising sheer on all four sides. It was a small, claustrophobic area about twenty paces by twenty paces and most of it was filled by a large wooden structure that I recognized as a gallows. This was another place that I hadn't seen during my training. It was Execution Square—the place haunted by Netty!

"Yes, boy, this is where the condemned get their necks stretched! It's a grim place.

But over there is what we've come to see." Colne pointed to the furthest corner of the square, and we passed the gallows and halted about four paces away from an imposing iron door with a massive lock. I could hear water trickling in the near distance.

"This is the entrance to the Witch Well, and behind that door you'd face your worst nightmare. Don't ever go through there, and just be glad you're not in my shoes!"

3

On the Stroke of Midnight

After a week or so, I began to feel a lot better about being on the night shift. The duties were much easier than I'd been trained for because it wasn't necessary to feed the prisoners. Only the prisoner in the Witch Well got fed at night and that was Adam Colne's job. The other inmates were mostly sleeping or groaning or crying. You just had to patrol the corridors, and after a few days, I actually got used to the noises the prisoners made. I even made friends with one of the other guards—Samuel his name was. First friend I'd had in a very long time.

I never saw the ghost of Netty on my shift, but I suspected that she came close at times. Once I felt someone touch the back of my neck. It felt like the tip of an ice-cold finger. But when I turned to look, there was nobody there—or at least nothing that needed to draw breath. There were whispers too but very faint, and I never could quite make out the words. Samuel never heard anything, but then he hadn't been chosen by Netty.

I would have been all right and probably still doing that job but then the Purple Pestilence came along and changed everything for a while.

The disease swept straight through the nearby villages and towns. Some people got sore throats so severe that they couldn't breathe. Then, just before they died, they turned a deep purple color. It was mostly the very young and the very old who died, but the survivors had a very hard time of it too and were confined to their sick beds for weeks. The orphanage didn't escape. Mrs. Hendle succumbed to it and so did a dozen of the weaker lads. I was glad to be away from the place at night.

One night I went to the castle and Adam Colne wasn't there. Three other guards were sick too—Samuel included. That left just me and George, the gate guard.

"Well, boy, this is a bad situation," he told me. "That prisoner in the Witch Well has to be fed at midnight, and with no Adam here, you'll have to do it."

"Me?" I said. "But I'm still new. Mr. Colne said I should never go into the Witch Well."

"Look, there's only you available to do it tonight, boy. I can't afford to leave the gate," he argued.

I knew that anyone could guard the gate but, although George was older and more experienced than I was, he was scared to feed the prisoner and was using the gate as an excuse.

"Couldn't we just leave it for one night?" I suggested. "Mr. Colne might be back tomorrow."

"It will go worse for everyone if that thing's not fed, boy. That's as much as I know. And that's what they pay you for."

I wasn't going to win this argument. "Where's the food?" I asked, my knees knocking just at the very thought of entering the Witch Well.

"There are two buckets waiting for you in Execution Square, directly underneath the gallows. Give the prisoner the first at midnight then the second course about ten minutes later. Just tip each bucket down the steps. Don't linger. Get out of there just as quickly as you can."

"Ten minutes later," I repeated. "All right, I'll do it."

"Good boy. Now, off you go on your rounds, but when you hear the church bell sound at a quarter to midnight, make your way to the Witch Well."

So, carrying my big bunch of keys, I set off on my patrol of the corridors. I was really scared—and lonely too, with no other guard to talk to. I just wanted to get the ordeal over with and I was actually glad when I heard the church bell in the distance telling me that it was time to go and feed the prisoner. Between the main gate and Execution Square, there were seven corridors to walk and eight stout doors to unlock and lock. At last I reached the square. It was raining even harder than usual and I picked my way between the puddles toward the gallows to where the two large wooden buckets of food were waiting.

Each was covered with a piece of wood to stop the rain getting in, and there was a stone on top to keep the wood in place. Why the stone was necessary I hadn't a clue. The four sheer walls that enclosed the gallows meant there could be no wind.

In the distance the church bell began to toll again. At the twelfth peal, I picked up the nearest bucket and carried it toward the door of the Witch Well. The bucket was so heavy. What on earth could be inside it? I lowered it to one side of the gate and fumbled for the right key. The lock seemed stiff, but at last it yielded and very nervously I pulled open the door.

There was a torch flickering on the wall just to the side of the door. It lit the entrance adequately, but the steps descended into absolute darkness. With one hand on the doorjamb, I listened. For a moment I could hear nothing at all, but then from far below came the faint sound of breathing.

I lifted the stone from the wooden cover of the bucket and placed it on the floor. Next I removed the cover itself. I was instantly assailed by a strong metallic coppery smell. The bucket was full of blood. Rich dark blood. Surely this wasn't food intended for a human being? What kind of creature could be imprisoned below? Mr. Colne had said he was chained up. But what was he?

I didn't intend to linger long enough to find out, so I did as the gatekeeper had instructed. I lifted the heavy bucket and I

tipped it, allowing the contents to cascade down the stone steps. The blood flowed like a waterfall, carrying big chunks of raw meat along with it.

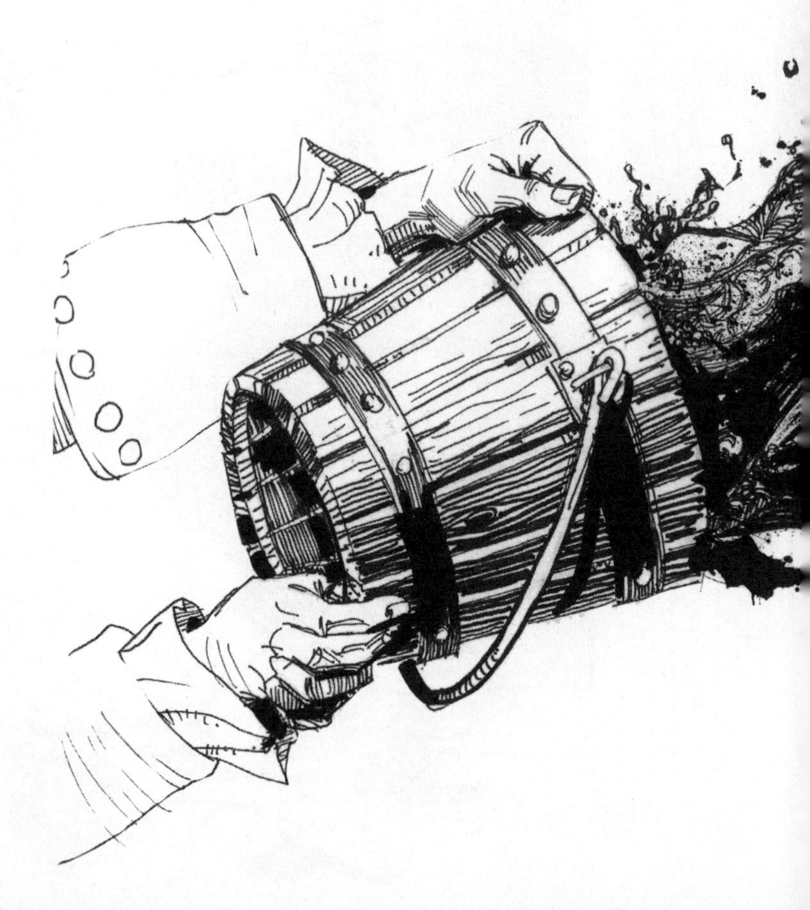

Wasting no time, I carried the empty bucket outside, closed the door behind me, and locked it. As instructed I waited ten minutes before getting ready to feed the creature what the gatekeeper had called its "second course." At one point I thought

I could hear faint noises from behind the door, so I leaned against it and put my ear to the wood. I could definitely hear chewing, snuffling noises, but after a while all became quiet and I judged it time to unlock the door and feed the prisoner again. I was more nervous than ever. What if he was lying in wait for me behind the door? I eased it open.

To my relief, it was exactly as before, the steps leading down into absolute darkness. The only difference was that the stones were now red with blood. A sudden thought struck me. They had been clean before I'd tipped the first bucket. So who had done it? Was that part of Adam Colne's job too? Was I going to have to scrub these steps when I'd finished?

This second bucket was also filled almost to the brim with blood, so wasting no time at all, I tipped it down the steps. It proved to be different from the first course; this had bones in it rather than pieces of raw meat. I turned, intending to get out of there fast. It was then that disaster struck.

I heard the door behind me creak on its hinges.

Then it started to close!

I took two quick steps toward the door but it slammed shut in my face. There had been no wind, so why had it closed? It was almost as if someone had shut it from the outside. Shut me in! When I tried to push the door open, it didn't yield and I began to panic, an iciness coursing through my veins. But there was worse to come.

Then I remembered with a sickening jolt that I'd left my key in the lock! In my nervousness to tip the second bucket down the steps and

get the job over with, I'd broken an important rule.

To my horror and dismay, I heard the sound of the key being turned in the lock. I tried to push open the door again, but it wouldn't budge. Someone had locked it. *But who could have done it and why?*

4

The Prisoner in the Witch Well

Now I was trapped in the Witch Well with the prisoner. A prisoner who drank blood and ate bones and had to be chained up! I could hear him somewhere below starting to eat his second course.

First there came the lapping and slurping of a big tongue drinking the blood that I'd poured down the stone steps.

How big is the tongue? No human tongue could make so much noise!

Next there came the crunching, grinding of large teeth chewing the bones that had been carried down to him by the red tide.

How big and sharp are the teeth? No human teeth could chew through bones like that!

I tried the door for the third time, again without success. Who had done this to me? It couldn't be George. I was doing him a favor feeding this creature. Could it be one of the prisoners? But no, I'd just checked them. They were all safe, under lock and key.

I sat down, resting my back against the door, thinking desperately about what I

could do. It was no good shouting for help because the gatekeeper was too far away. And if I did call out, the prisoner below me would certainly hear and might come up the steps to investigate.

The gatekeeper wouldn't expect me back until the end of my shift. It was only then, when the day guards arrived, that someone might discover my disappearance and come to release me from the Witch Well. But that was still many hours away.

Maybe if I stayed at the top of the steps, quiet as a little mouse, the prisoner would stay down there. No sooner had that thought entered my head than the chewing below ceased. The prisoner must have eaten all the bones. *Perhaps he's now full to bursting and will fall asleep?*

That hope was quickly shattered. There

was a new sound, like a broad-toothed file rasping on wood. *What could it be?*

The sound went on for a long time and seemed to be getting gradually nearer and nearer. There was also the occasional clank of a chain. Something deep inside my brain figured out what the noises meant, and the answer popped into my head very suddenly. As the truth dawned on me, I started to tremble.

The creature was slowly climbing the steps and dragging its chain behind it. The rasping sound was being made by its large tongue. Nobody needed to clean the steps of blood because the prisoner did it himself. He was climbing upward, licking each step in turn, not wanting to waste even a drop of blood. Climbing upward—toward *me*!

I had one hope left. A lot depended on the

length of the chain that tethered him to the ring in the dungeon below. It seemed sensible to me for the prison authorities to have made it long enough so he could reach the top step with his tongue—that would save on the need to send in someone to do the cleaning—but not long enough to allow him to reach the door. That way anyone feeding him would be safe as long as they stood very close to the entrance.

But if that was the case, why had the gatekeeper told me to get out as quickly as possible? Was there some other danger that I hadn't foreseen?

The sound of that tongue licking the step was getting nearer and nearer, and I stood up and pressed my back against the door to get as far as possible from the top step. Next, I braced myself, ready for my first view of the creature. I didn't have long to wait. The first thing to emerge into the light cast by the flickering torch was the tongue itself. It was huge and swollen and also purple, like the faces of those who died from the pestilence.

Next came the huge head, and I shuddered at the sight of it. Rather than hair, it was covered in green scales and its ears were long and pointy, with a sharp piece of bone

protruding from the tip of each. What *was* it?

As more of the prisoner came into view, I gradually became aware of its size. It was far bigger than a man, perhaps nine feet tall, with strong muscular shoulders and a naked, hairy

back. Instead of fingernails, it had long, sharp talons, each one more lethal than a dagger.

Its tongue was licking the top step now and so absorbed was the creature in slurping up every last drop of blood that, so far, it hadn't noticed me. My heart was in my mouth and I pressed myself even harder back against the door.

But the moment it finished, it looked up and its big, green, cruel eyes looked directly into mine. For the first time, I saw its teeth. It had two long, yellow fangs that curled down over its bottom lip. With a snarl, it leaped toward me. The chain brought it up with a jerk and it thrashed against the metal, straining to reach me, its claws just inches from my shoes, saliva dribbling from its open mouth in anticipation of eating my flesh. *Would the chain hold?*

Now I didn't worry about keeping quiet. I didn't care who heard me. "George!" I screamed, banging on the solid door. "George, please, help me! Somebody help!"

But if anyone heard me, they didn't come. I stopped banging on the door and turned to face the creature. He growled deep in his throat. For a moment I waited, trembling in dread, expecting one of the big links of his chain to break. But they remained intact and the creature's attempts to reach me slowly became less frantic. I tried to remain calm.

The only risk to my life was if I grew tired and fell forward, away from the door. But I was hardly likely to fall asleep with the hungry, open, fanged mouth of that monstrosity a few feet away and its claws mere inches from my shoes. Colne had said he'd lost guards in the Witch Well. But I didn't intend to be another victim.

Slowly my fear began to ebb. I told myself that I could survive here until daybreak. But then, just as I was becoming calmer and more hopeful, there was a sudden draft and the torch began to flicker. The draft became a gust, the gust became a howling wind, and the torch went out. I was plunged into darkness.

5

Long-Necked Netty

For a moment I could see nothing, and then there was a faint glow from the side of the steps. The glow became a tall column of light that lit the walls and steps better than a candle, and a human form began to materialize.

My heart started to beat faster. This was one of the castle ghosts and it only took a few moments for me to realize which one. At first glance, the body looked solid and the red lips, brown eyes, and green dress could have fooled you into thinking that this was a living flesh-and-blood woman. But she was standing in front of the creature from the dungeon, and I could see through her to his glaring eyes and twitching talons.

She was a tall woman who once had been

beautiful, but the high cheekbones and glossy black hair were ruined by two things: her bulging eyes and her stretched and twisted neck with its knotted veins. I shuddered with fear. It was the ghost of Long-Neck Netty, the woman who'd been hanged in the castle's Execution Square.

Netty smiled without warmth and then she spoke; her voice was as cold as the north wind. "*Billy Calder, we meet at last. I see you've met my son. So what do you think of him?*" she asked.

I didn't answer, and she turned and gestured toward the taloned creature on the steps who was straining against the chain, making fresh efforts to reach me. "*He's a good lad and deserves the best,*" she said. "*He didn't ask to be born in that shape and he's always hungry. It was my fault, you see. I met a young man, the most handsome that*

any woman had ever seen. He had blue eyes and curly blond hair, not unlike yourself, and a dazzling smile that melted my heart. I'd have done anything for him."

Why was she telling me all this? What did she want?

"But I was young and foolish," she continued, *"and never questioned the fact that he only ever wanted to meet me after dark and alone. I was a witch but I was self-taught and belonged to no coven, so I had no one to advise me and point out the great danger that I was in. I bore a child to that handsome young man, and it was only afterward that I learned the truth. He was the Devil! And some offspring of a witch and the Devil are born as abhumans. My poor child, he never asked to be brought into this world so ugly and misshapen, so I try to make it up to him whenever I can. I feed him a choice morsel,*

some tender flesh and sweet young blood. That's why you are here, boy. That's why I asked for you to be transferred to the night shift! You aren't the first young lad I've asked Adam Colne to bring my way. He daren't refuse me or he'd be given to my son instead! Oh, I know he tries to warn you boys, but I always find a way of getting you in the end."

My blood froze and my brain screamed with terror. From the moment that she had demanded I be moved to the night shift, her intention had been to feed me to her son.

"Why don't you make it easy for yourself?" Netty cried. *"Just walk down the steps and get it over with. The pain won't last long!"*

I was too terrified to reply. But I still had hope. She was just a ghost, and although she could scare me, Netty couldn't actually make me do anything. I could still wait at the top of

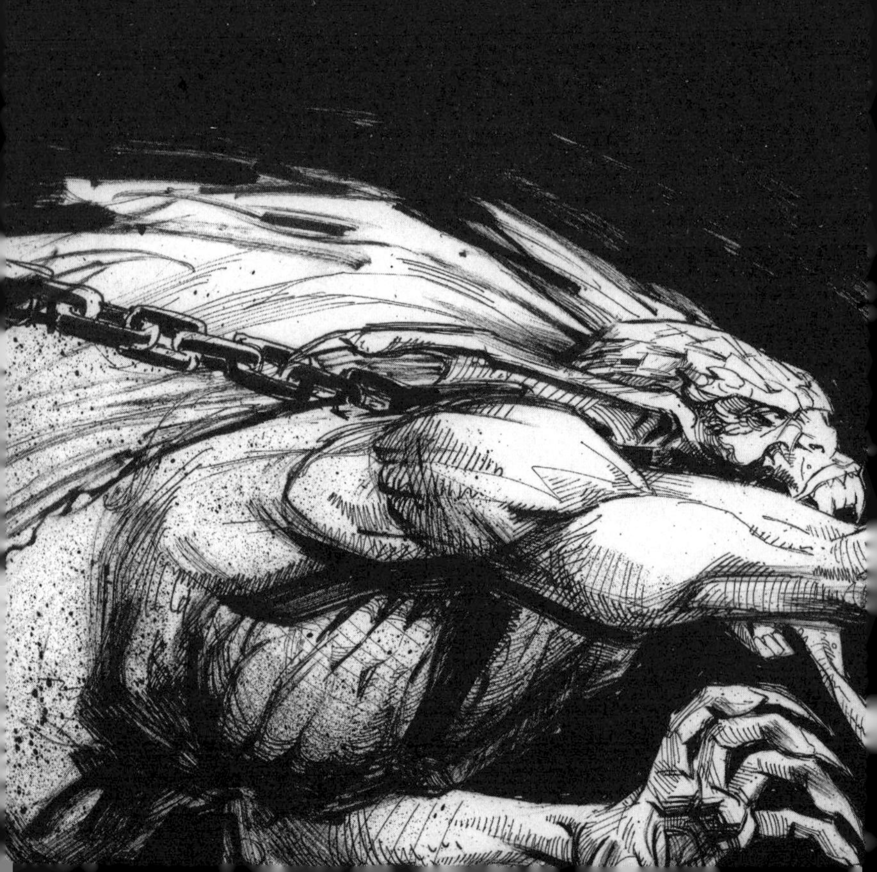

the steps until someone from the day shift came to unlock the door and set me free.

"Do we have to do it the hard way? Do I have to drag you down the steps?"

"You're just a ghost!" I shouted, my knees trembling. "You have no substance. You can't drag me anywhere!"

"Oh! Can't I, boy? You don't know very much about ghosts, do you? Who do you think turned the key and locked you in here?"

Netty moved closer and

stretched out her left hand toward me until her ghostly fingers were touching my neck. I could actually feel her cold fingertips! Then there was a sudden tug at the collar of my shirt, and for a moment I lost my balance. I tottered at the top of the steps and almost pitched forward into the waiting talons of the abhuman. He was straining against the chain again, slavering in anticipation of eating my flesh and drinking my blood.

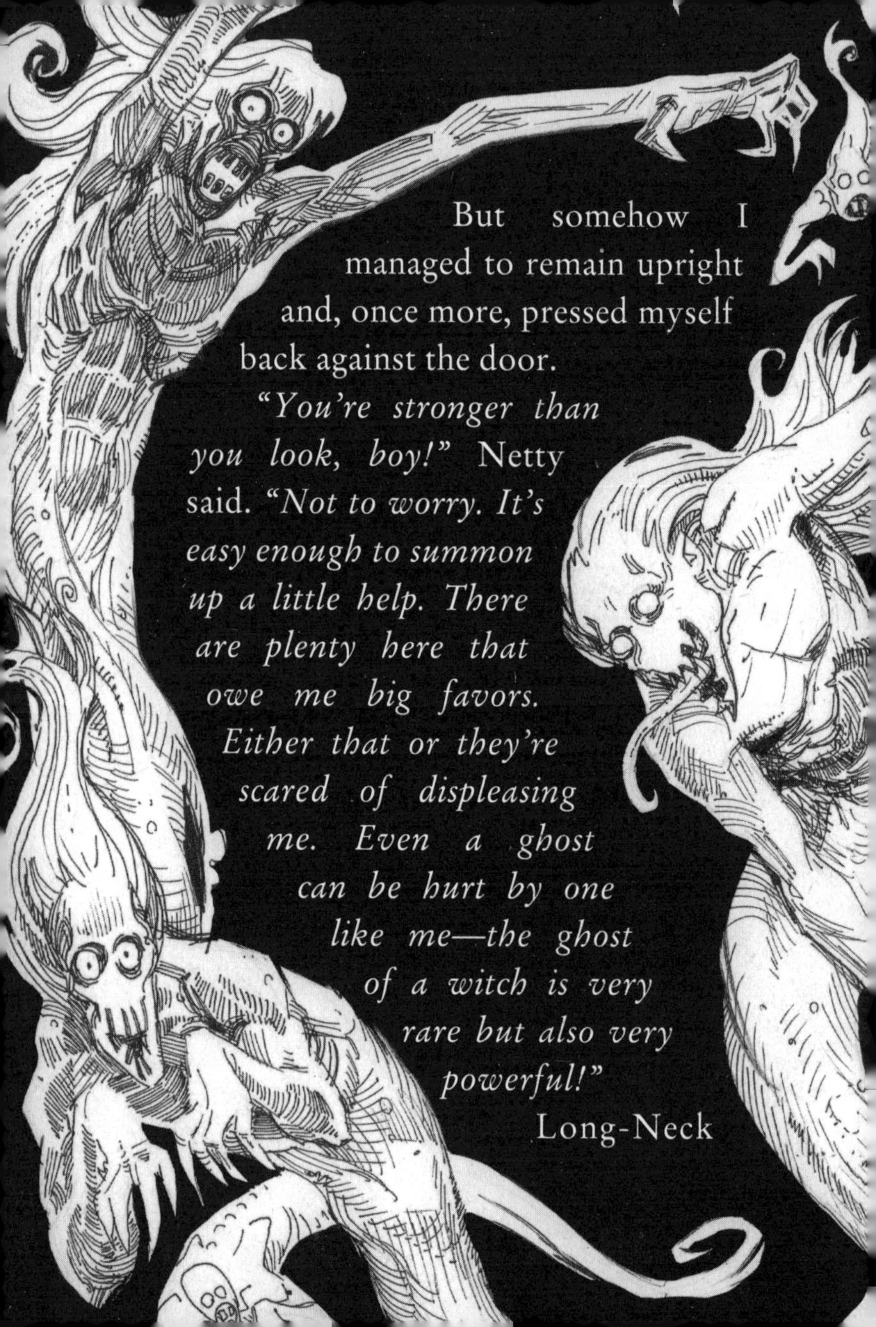

But somehow I managed to remain upright and, once more, pressed myself back against the door.

"*You're stronger than you look, boy!*" Netty said. "*Not to worry. It's easy enough to summon up a little help. There are plenty here that owe me big favors. Either that or they're scared of displeasing me. Even a ghost can be hurt by one like me—the ghost of a witch is very rare but also very powerful!*"

Long-Neck

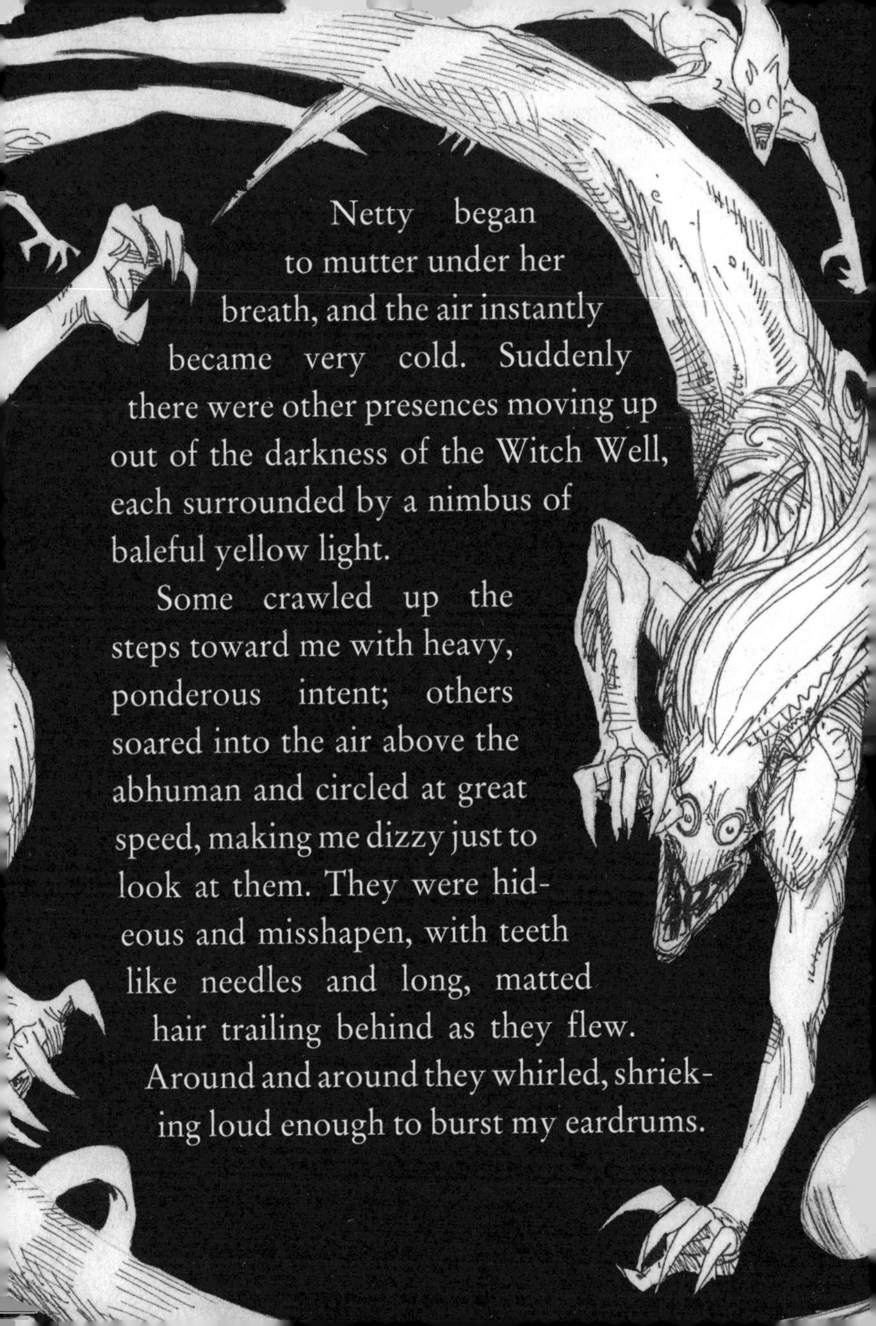

Netty began to mutter under her breath, and the air instantly became very cold. Suddenly there were other presences moving up out of the darkness of the Witch Well, each surrounded by a nimbus of baleful yellow light.

Some crawled up the steps toward me with heavy, ponderous intent; others soared into the air above the abhuman and circled at great speed, making me dizzy just to look at them. They were hideous and misshapen, with teeth like needles and long, matted hair trailing behind as they flew. Around and around they whirled, shrieking loud enough to burst my eardrums.

Then they began to tug at my clothes and pinch my skin with their sharp fingernails.

"Get away from me!" I screamed, hitting out in all directions. Netty cackled and chortled, loving every second of my desperate struggle. I fought to keep my balance, but the castle ghosts were relentless and their attempts to tug me down the stone steps went on and on, while Netty grinned at me and her son drooled in anticipation of the feast to come.

But I was determined to survive. I just had to hang on for a few hours. Help would eventually arrive. I could do it!

Never give up! I told myself. *Never give up!*

Freedom

All that happened a long time ago and my memories of that terrible experience have now faded somewhat. I've walked the corridors of the castle for many years now, and I've gotten used to the ghosts, so most of them don't scare me that much anymore. In fact, Adam Colne was right—they've almost become a family to me, replaced the family I lost a long time ago. But I always stay away from the Witch Well; it still doesn't do to get too close to Long-Neck Netty and her abhuman son.

Guards come and go. Samuel and George are long gone and Adam Colne has retired—his son has taken his place. It seems to be a family tradition. Four generations of Colnes

have guarded the Witch Well. No doubt I'll still be around when Adam's grandson takes over. I'll be here as long as the walls of the castle still stand. I know my place in the scheme of things.

Because now I'm one of the castle ghosts.

About the Author

Do I believe in ghosts?

I do believe in ghosts. I certainly think that I once heard one.

In Combe Martin, Devon, I stayed at a hotel called the Pack o' Cards which is supposed to be haunted by a white lady.

In the middle of the night there were strange disturbing noises. It began with a pattering under the floorboards which I tried to convince myself was just mice. If so those mice had big feet! Then suddenly

there was a very loud noise which was difficult to explain. It sounded as if a heavy coin had been chucked into a large metal bucket and that sound reverberated right down through the bedroom floor. Things that go clang in the night are really scary! There was little sleep to be had after that...

Joseph Delaney

About the Illustrator

Do I believe in ghosts?

This is a true story. I was ten years old and alone in my long deceased great-grandparents' house in upstate New York. There are many family stories about the strange happenings in that house and they made me avoid being there by myself, normally.

But I was upstairs on my own, sitting in the bathroom, reading a comic book. When nature calls, one must answer! So I'd left the game of tag with my cousins in the yard to answer that call. First, I heard the floorboards creaking in the hall. Then the sound of foot-steps, each one very distinct, approached and stopped just outside the closed bathroom door. "Someone's in here!" I called out. No one answered. The door had a small brass knob. Sitting here at age forty, I can still remember that knob vividly—tarnished with a raised ridge around its circumference. I can especially remember watching the knob turn, the click of the latch, and the groaning hinges as the door swung open, exposing me to the house in a most vulnerable way.

But there was no one there. I could see all of my cousins through the bathroom window still playing in the yard. My trousers were barely done up as I burst out the front door, screaming...

Scott M. Fischer

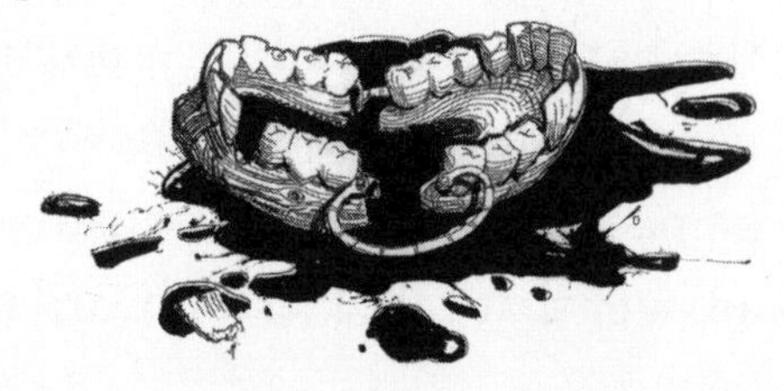